DINO-RACING

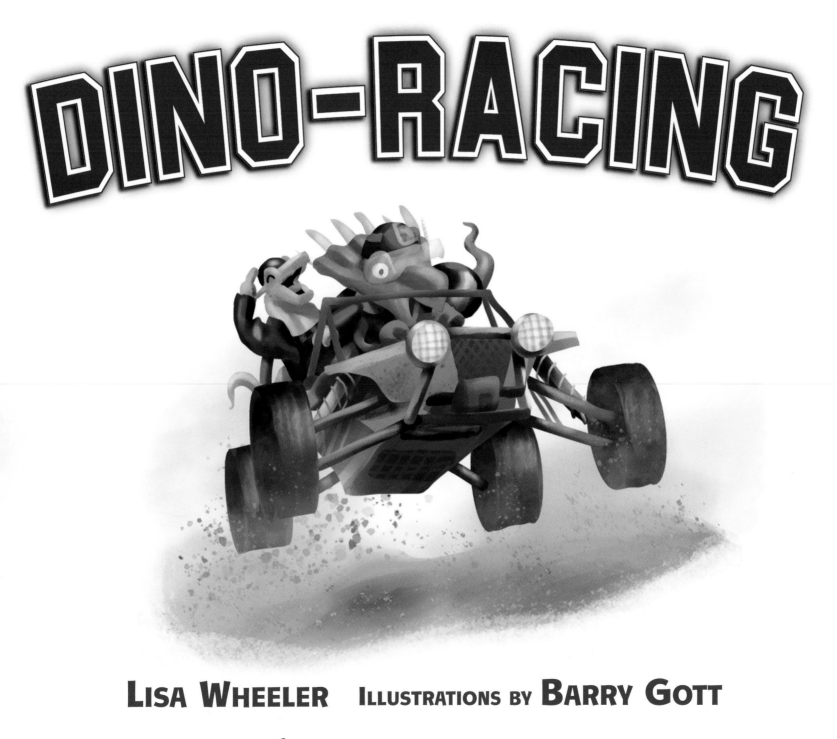

LISA WHEELER   **ILLUSTRATIONS BY BARRY GOTT**

CAROLRHODA BOOKS MINNEAPOLIS

To my friend, David Hess, who
loves NASCAR —L.W.

To Rose, Finn, and Nandi —B.G.

Carolrhoda Books
A division of Lerner Publishing Group, Inc.
241 First Avenue North
Minneapolis, MN 55401 USA

For reading levels and more information, look up this title at www.lernerbooks.com.

Design by Emily Harris.
Main body text set in Churchward Samoa 22/36.
Typeface provided by BlueHead Studio.
The illustrations in this book were created in Adobe
Illustrator and Photoshop and Corel Painter.

Library of Congress Cataloging-in-Publication Data

Names: Wheeler, Lisa, 1963- author.
Title: Dino-racing / by Lisa Wheeler.
Description: Minneapolis : Carolrhoda Books, [2016] | Summary:
    Illustrations and rhyming text follow dinosaurs as they race against
    each other in dragsters, then off-road vehicles, and finally stock cars.
Identifiers: LCCN 2015037128| ISBN 9781512403145 (lb : alk. paper) |
    ISBN 9781512408867 (eb pdf)
Subjects: | CYAC: Stories in rhyme. | Dinosaurs—Fiction. | Automobile
    racing—Fiction. | Racing—Fiction.
Classification: LCC PZ8.3.W5668 Dil 2016 | DDC [E]—dc23

LC record available at https://lccn.loc.gov/2015037128

Manufactured in the United States of America
2-43727-21079-2/8/2017

See the happy dino faces
heading to the auto races!

Fans are ready for some speed.
They hope their favorite cars succeed.

This event will make them smile:
a drag race down the quarter mile!

Allo's wearing red with pride—
her top-fuel dragster by her side.

Stego's car is blazing green
with stickers touting *Dino-Kleen!*

The drivers look like safety models:
helmets, jumpsuits, gloves, and goggles.

Drag-strip lanes are long and straight.
Both the drivers sit and wait.

They watch the post with lights aglow:
two green beacons tell them . . .

PRE-STAGE

STAGE

. . . GO!

Down the strip in record time—
who'll be the first to cross the line?

PRE-STAGE

STAGE

Milliseconds will decide.

Parachutes then open wide.

Special cameras catch the action.

"*Allo* wins it by a fraction!"

Next, the desert comes alive:
this off-road race needs all-wheel drive!

Maia has an all-girl crew.
Each one knows just what to do.

With compass, road book, GPS,
Pachy navigates the best.

In the green truck, **Minmi's** *chasing*,
hauling tools and gear for racing.

Raptor wants a repeat win—
high-fives his crew, the **Ptero Twins**.

Teams are ready, drivers rested.
Off-road skills will soon be tested.

All the buggies are equipped
with cages (just in case they flip).

This race will last for three whole days.
"Let's get this rally under way!"

The race goes on for miles and miles
through dunes and drifts and rocky piles.

Raptor hits the rhythm section,
glad his ride has good suspension.

Suddenly, his buggy tilts!

Now, his front end's stuck in silt.

The **Ptero Twins** will save the day.

Hook up the winch! He's on his way!

Maia strikes a hidden rock!

Her axle breaks. She has to stop.

Minmi comes to lend a hand.

Soon they're racing 'cross the sand.

The checkpoint is around the bend—
still many miles before the end.

Time cards stamped. Fuel up, then rest.
Sun is setting in the west.

Tonight they park their trucks and cars
and sleep below the twinkling stars.

After days of highs and lows,
the rally's coming to a close.

Times and stages are considered.
Points and penalties are figured.

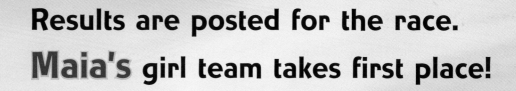

Results are posted for the race.
Maia's girl team takes first place!

	MAGULODON
G MAIASAURUS	UTAHRAPTOR
SUCHOM...	...LOSAURUS
TARBOSAU...	...OSAURUS
VULCANODO...	...SAURUS
TROODON	...IMUS
MUSSASAURU...	...VITHOLUS
PENTACERATO...	...TOR

Over to the stock-car track:
It's oval-shaped, high-banked, and black.

Dino-racing fans are here.
Excitement's in the atmosphere!

Cars line up—a double row.

The green flag signals, *Go! Go! Go!*

Out front, as everyone expects,
our reigning champ—the King—**T-Rex**!

The cars move like a rolling herd.
Diplo, second. Compy, third.

Galli's in fifth, drafting behind
Tricera in fourth—cars aligned.

Counterclockwise, forty laps . . .
when **T-Rex** feels a sudden tap!

He fishtails right. Slides like a sled.
That's when **Diplo** pulls ahead!

Down the straightaway he zooms.

Then **Compy** hollers, *"Make some room!"*

That carnivore shows no restraint.

Side by side, they're trading paint!

Tricera's in the pit-stop lane.
His racing tires need a change.

Clean the windshield. Add some gas.
Eleven seconds? Wow! That's fast!

Back in the race with hopes to lead,
he's cautious as he picks up speed—

steers clear of spinouts, crashes, fires,
breakdowns, bumps, and rolling tires.

Tricera sees the end in sight.
He passes Galli on the right.

Ahead are Diplo and T-Rex.
The crowd goes wild! What happens next?

Foot on the gas. Determined face . . .

. . . **Triceratops** has won the race!

In Victory Lane—third, second, and first!
Tricera thinks his heart might burst.

The trophy's big. His smile is wide,
his crew and family by his side.

Overcome, he sheds a tear.
Racing's over, but never fear . . .

Dino-dancing is finally here!